Carolyn Wells, Claude F. Bragdon

At the Sign of the Sphinx

a book of charades

Carolyn Wells, Claude F. Bragdon

At the Sign of the Sphinx
a book of charades

ISBN/EAN: 9783337388348

Printed in Europe, USA, Canada, Australia, Japan

Cover: Foto ©Andreas Hilbeck / pixelio.de

More available books at **www.hansebooks.com**

At the SIGN of the SPHINX

A BOOK OF CHARADES

By CAROLYN WELLS

"I'll put another question to thee; if thou answerest not to the purpose, confess thyself—"

HAMLET, V. I.

NEW YORK, *Published by* STONE AND KIMBALL *in the year* M DCCC XCVI

To

DR. WILLIAM J. ROLFE,

"The dearest friend to me, the kindest man,
The best-condition'd and unwearied spirit
In doing courtesies."

THIS BOOK IS DEDICATE.

PROOFS.

THE figures indicate the number of letters in each syllable of the answer, as the word is divided in Webster's Dictionary ; but not necessarily as it is divided in the Charade.

1	. . . . 4, 4	23	. . . . 4, 3
2	. . . . 3, 4	24	. . . . 4, 4
3	. . . . 3, 3	25	. . . . 4, 6
4	. . . . 4, 2	26	. . . . 5, 4
5	. . . . . 3, 2, 4	27	. . . . 4, 3
6	. . . . 4, 4	28	. . . . 4, 5
7	. . . . . 3, 2, 3	29	. . . . 5, 5
8	. . . . 2, 4, 1, 4	30	. . . . 4, 3
9	. . . . 3, 5	31	. . . . 2, 4
10	. . . . 3, 3	32	. . . . 4, 3
11	. . . . 2, 4	33	. . . . 4, 4
12	. . . . 2, 5	34	. . . . 3, 4
13	. . . . 2, 3	35	. . . . 4, 2
14	. . . . 4, 4	36	. . . . . 3, 2, 3
15	. . . . 3, 3	37	. . . . 3, 4
16	. . . . 5, 5	38	. . . . 4, 4
17	. . . . 3, 5	39	. . . . 4, 5
18	. . . . 5, 4	40	. . . . 3, 4
19	. . . . 4, 4	41	. . . . 4, 2
20	. . . . 4, 4	42	. . . . 2, 3
21	. . . . 3, 3	43	. . . . 3, 4
22	. . . . 3, 4	44	. . . . 4, 3

45	. . . . . . 5, 3	73	. . . . . . 4, 3
46	. . . . . . 4, 4	74	. . . . . . 2, 4
47	. . . . . . 2, 4	75	. . . . . . 3, 5
48	. . . . . . 2, 3	76	. . . . . . 4, 3
49	. . . . . . 2, 3	77	. . . . . . 3, 4
50	. . . . . . 4, 2	78	. . . . . . 5, 4
51	. . . . . . 3, 3	79	. . . . . . 4, 5
52	. . . . . 2, 2, 3	80	. . . . . . 2, 4
53	. . . . . . 4, 4	81	. . . . . . 2, 2
54	. . . . . . 4, 4	82	. . . . . . 5, 4
55	. . . . . . 3, 2	83	. . . . . . 2, 4
56	. . . . . . 3, 4	84	. . . . . . 2, 5
57	. . . . . . 4, 5	85	. . . . . . 3, 5
58	. . . . . . 4, 5	86	. . . . . . 4, 4
59	. . . . . . 3, 4	87	. . . . . . 4, 5
60	. . . . . . 5, 4	88	. . . . . 4, 2, 3
61	. . . . . . 5, 4	89	. . . . . . 4, 4
62	. . . . . . 2, 5	90	. . . . . . 5, 3
63	. . . . . . 3, 4	91	. . . . . . 3, 4
64	. . . . . . 6, 4	92	. . . . . . 5, 4
65	. . . . . . 5, 3	93	. . . . . . 3, 3
66	. . . . . 4, 3, 5	94	. . . . . . 4, 4
67	. . . . . 3, 3, 4	95	. . . . . . 3, 4
68	. . . . . 2, 2, 3	96	. . . . . . 3, 4
69	. . . . . . 4, 4	97	. . . . . . 4, 4
70	. . . . . . 4, 4	98	. . . . . . 1, 4
71	. . . . . 3, 3, 4	99	. . . . . . 5, 5
72	. . . . . . 3, 3		

I

MY first, what power and might are
thine !
Sometimes I think thou art divine ;
Titled and great ! we often see
A shrinking culprit brought to thee.

My second, fond of fruit and flowers,
Thou lovest to bide in leafy bowers ;
Yet, heeding not the solemn gloom,
Thou visitest the hero's tomb.

My whole, though by my whole accursed,
Each day buys and devours my first.

2

THE sunset's golden glowing
    Fades from the Western skies ;
In dreamy silence, rowing,
    I watch my first arise.

The mystic shadows, stealing,
    Bring thrills I dare not name ;
I tremble slightly, feeling
    My last through all my frame.

My oars I swiftly feather :
    It is my whole, these nights
Of cool September weather,
    To seek my boat's delights.

3

IN tropic trees the agile apes my first from
    limb to limb ;
And ancient history says my second's head
    was made to swim ;
And for the culminating point, my whole's a
    synonym.

4

WHEN the golden day is waking,
    And night's shadows are dispersed,
Then the lark, the silence breaking,
    Sweetly warbles forth my first.

Many a shining fate we 've beckoned,
    Failing often, hoping still
That my second and my second
    Our desires we may fulfil.

Total is a book. We find it
    Just a little past its prime;
And departing leaves behind it
    Footprints on the sands of time.

5

THERE was a sound of revelry by night,
　　And stealthily my first came to my
　　　whole
　　Upon my third.　The moon was shining
　　　bright,
　　　And others came.　Their voices stirred
　　　my soul.
　　No sleep till morn!　Unless with missile
　　　fleet
　　I chase my first away with flying feet.
　　Though to my second in my aim I
　　　feared,
　　After a few attempts they disappeared.

6

U P from the South at break of day
My first arrived in early May,
And through the towns and cities passed,
Heralded by a trumpet blast.

Up from the South my total came,
Up from the land of flowery fame ;
And reached my second's sheltering care,
After a voyage long and fair.

7

WITHIN my hammock, alone and lazy,
  Through smoke-wreaths hazy I see
    my friend ;
In calm contentment at home abiding,
  I watch him striding around the bend.

Across the meadow among the thistles
  He sings and whistles in careless glee;
He does not heed me, I know he 's
    going
  Where streams are flowing to one,
    two, three.

I give my mind up to idle fancies,
  Such as a man sees in sunny Spain,
A half-forgotten pastime in Seville,
  A pictured revel forms in my brain.

A Spanish maid decked with scarlet
    roses,
  Whose swaying poses delight like
    rhyme
Dainty and graceful, her bright eyes
    glancing
  While to her dancing my whole
    keeps time.

8

THE empty shell is always worthless named
After my first's outcast ;
A contract often is my next proclaimed
After a time has passed ;
" God bless us every one ! " my third
exclaimed,
After he did my last.
When you have guessed the total word,
You will declare it is my third.

9

MY first's a term in golfing, though in
that I'm not much versed ;
My first is in my second, when my
second's in my first.
And when my whole is in my first,
my first is in my whole,
And when my first is in my last, we
quaff its flowing bowl.

THERE was once a merry maiden, a
      bewitching, gay brunette;
   In the art of breaking hearts she was
      well versed;
And she flirted and coquetted with every
      man she met,
   Until everybody said it was my first.

When the lovers flocked around her, and
      sought her smiles to win,
   And at her dainty feet their fortunes
      cast,
She flouted them, and scouted them, to
      their intense chagrin,
   While heartlessly she chuckled in my
      last.

But one by one her suitors grew impatient
      of her ways,
   And one by one escaped from her
      control;
Until none of her devoted slaves remained,
      and all her days
   The lonely little maiden lived my whole.

II

OFTEN with dread and horror seen,
Although sometimes proclaimed a queen,
My first with no intent of ill
Began the battle of Bunker Hill.

My second is a growing thing,
We welcome it anew each spring;
'T is eaten gladly by the cow,
I think you 're looking at it now.

The differing creeds, it seems to me,
On this one point will all agree :
That he who wants to save his soul
Must honestly profess my whole.

12

SWEET Priscilla at my side,
Gayly o'er the waves we ride.
As we banter on the yacht,
She is happy, I am not;
For beneath my first, her eyes
Frown and smile and tantalize.
Though she rules my very soul,
She is governed by my whole.
If she 'd only marry me,
How contented I would be;
If I heard our wedding-bell,
If my second on us fell,
Gayly then away I 'd ride
Sweet Priscilla at my side.

13

MY first was set before a king;
My second is a piece of ground;
When I my ship to land would bring
I like to have my whole around.

14

ON either side the river lie
Long fields of barley and of rye;
My first blows free beneath the sky,
And through the field the road runs by
    To many-towered Camelot.

There she weaves by night and day
A magic web of colors gay;
She dare not from my second stray,
    The Lady of Shalott.

The gemmy bridle glittered free,
Like to some branch of stars we see;
Perhaps it was my whole to thee,
    O bold Sir Lancelot!

15

I AM my whole.   I have been married twice.
My first wife was my second long before
My second wife became my first.   And
more,
I was my whole to each.   Let that suffice.

16

YOU see my first when you behold
   The jester's broadly grinning face.
Proud of his skill, the huntsman bold
   Brings home my second from the chase.
Although my whole is cheap and mean,
I would not change with king or queen.

17

FIRST in my first was Washington;
　　No foe against him could prevail.
My second always is around,
　　But yet it keeps outside the pale.
My whole the Western pioneers
Shuddering heard with grewsome fears.

2

18

MY first, of thee the poets sing,
And notes of praise to thee they bring;
Though dark, yet fair thou 'rt said to be,
And many prayers ascend to thee.

My second, beautiful but shy,
Thou wilt with me this evening fly;
With cushioned cab, and thee beside,
Methinks I could forever ride.

My whole! what horrors dread are thine,
What fiendish tortures, deeds malign,
What ghastly terrors! yet from thee,
A word will set thy victims free.

19

EVEN in this enlightened day
Many a woman's first, they say,
   Beneath the yoke is seen ;
The yoke is of my second made ;
My heavy whole upon it laid
   Gleams with metallic sheen.

UNDER the shimmering starbeams bright,
   Gayly I rambled with Rosalie
In grandmother's garden that summer
   night.

With her eyes so blue, with her skin so
   white,
   With my first so red, she was fair to see,
Under the shimmering starbeams bright.

The mischievous moon shone with silver
   light
   As the maiden coquettishly smiled at me
In grandmother's garden that summer
   night.

Of all the village, she had the right
   To be called my second, I thought
   with glee,
Under the shimmering starbeams bright.

I plucked my total, so small and slight,
   And gave it to her as we wandered free
In grandmother's garden that summer
   night.

I was caught in her toils, the merry sprite!
I told her I loved her, on bended knee,
Under the shimmering starbeams bright,
In grandmother's garden that summer
night.

21

A CAT up out of the cellar stole,
And cautiously crept into my whole.
She thought, " I 'll last to reach that first,
So I can quench my awful thirst."
But the cook came in, and screamed out
    " Scat ! "
And out of my whole she cleared that cat.

22

WORSE than the wise men who sailed
    in a bowl,
A man in my first went over my
    whole;
And when he was found,
He was picked up, half drowned,
By my last which was sent out to bring
    him aground.

23

WHEN you have guessed my first,
    you 'll see
How very dear it is to me;
    With feathers soft and white and
    fair
It flutters in the evening air,
Marvel of grace and symmetry.

Jefferson, Edison, Hood, all three,
My second were well known to be;
    You 'll understand this, I declare,
        When you have guessed.

My whole is always said to flee
When shining day breaks o'er the lea;
    Its hollow laugh we 'll gladly spare,
    And gladly miss its ghostly glare;
To this I 'm sure you will agree
        When you have guessed.

24

HOW very clever he is reckoned
Who hits my first upon my second ;
And of all fools, he's deemed the worst
Who hits my second on my first ;
My whole was used to decorate
A Norman or a Gothic gate.

25

WE listened breathless, not a person
　　stirred;
The beating of my first we plainly
　　heard.
In life we often cross my last, when
　　dry,
But cross it wet when we are called
　　to die.
My whole will drive the neighbors
　　nearly wild;
It fell to my share when I was a
　　child.

26

MY first complains, " My hour is almost
        come
When I to sulphurous and tormenting
    flames
Must render up myself."
                        But from such fate
My last is safe.
                And though within the dark
And awful gloom of night I grope my
    way
To find my whole, when I have reached
    it, lo!
A sudden light illumines all the place.

27

AS my first trotted past,
   My second arose ;
For my total, aghast,
As my first trotted past,
Was discourteously cast
   On his poor little nose ;
As my first trotted past,
   My second arose.

28

L ONG in my first hath Cæsar lain,
And by my last a giant was slain.
My whole, with cold and silent ways,
Of grave demeanor, pithy phrase,
Yet given to flattery and praise.

29

BENEATH the sharp axe Queen Mary
knelt,
And often its blows my first has dealt
To kings and queens and chickens.

The hour for my whole to each must
come,
My first of my second is thought by some
The finest work of Dickens.

30

WHENEVER I take my walks abroad,
How many poor I see ;
Down in my first an awful fraud
This morning begged of me.
Each place I visited, revealed
Suffering and distress ;
I wandered homeward through a field,
My last clung to my dress.

Under thy influence, my whole,
Beneath thy absolute control,
Men cannot speak or sing or walk,
Or if they move around or talk,
By no volition of their own
They do it. But thy sway o'er-
thrown,
Then they resume their smiles and
tears,
Their joys and sorrows, hopes and
fears.

31

BENEATH my first a Cardinal dwelt,
And though unseen it may still be felt ;
The destroying angel o'er Israel passed,
When on their doorposts the blood was
　　　my last.
My whole its well-deserved punishment
　　　wins ;
It is one of the deadliest of sins.

3²

WHEN vows are made and troth is
    plighted,
'T is then we see my first united ;
My second, aye, and many such
Have known the handcuff's iron
    clutch ;

My whole's a busy travelling man ;
He 's been to China and Japan,
To Zanzibar and Timbuctoo,
To Paris, Pekin, and Peru.

33

MY first, men traverse land and sea,
In an untiring search for thee;
Yet thou art found in many boats,
From thee our flag in triumph floats.

Thee, my last, men will often thank,
A kind of fish, a badge of rank;
An actor who plays well his part,
Yet many wonder what thou art.

Far from their firesides and their wives,
My whole saved many sailors' lives,
Guided them safely, homeward bound;
In a bear's tail it may be found.

34

WHO first my last till they the bounds exceed,

Of my whole soon will surely stand in need.

35

MY gay-colored first is a bower
Which is spoiled if it's out in a shower;
    The heathen Chinee
    Was quick-witted to see
That it wields a remarkable power.

My last at Thermopylae fell,
For my last must be rung the death-
    knell;
    From fears that molest,
    My mind is at rest,
When my last they assure me is well.

My whole is a horrible beast
Which is found in the wilds of the East
    By Mr. Linnæus,
    Named Canis Aureus;
It is fond of the lately deceased.

36

MY first is part of a whizzing wheel; 't is made of iron or wood.

Of my second oft in fairy-tales we 've heard ;

He lives in darksome forests, and he wears a pointed hood.

And the capital of Nevada is my third.

My whole a Roman family once could claim,

But now, alas ! it 's nothing but a name.

37

IN a fair peach of glowing hue
My first is oft concealed from view;
My second, purple grapes supplies,
Cider and nuts and pumpkin-pies;
My total is a trap or snare
To catch the traveller unaware.

38

MY dainty first, I saw thee as I strayed
This morning by the brook. At dinner
now
Across the table, neatly washed and
dressed,
Fresh and piquant, I see thee once
again.
My second, as I gaze upon thy face
And note thy wreath of laurel and thy
shield,
I marvel not that thou hast mighty
power,
That thou art sought and cherished. By
thine aid
Churches are raised, houses and factories
built,
And many mills are thine. What won-
der, then,
We work for thee ? Thou art one sent
to us.
My whole, the pride and glory of the
Turks,
I watch thy graceful curves, and I
admire

Thy slender form.   When thou art
    older grown,
'T will be more full and round.   And
    then thou 'lt smile
Upon me from afar.

39

HO! fill your glass to comrades gay,
    Let song and laughter burst ;
Then fill your glass to those away,
    And fill it to my first.

Go bring a jug of my second up,
    Bring flagons of rare old wine,
And fetch the cherished loving-cup ;
    We 'll drink to mine and thine.

Now, who to mix this draught is skilled ?
    We want no bitter bowl
Like that which Dickens said was filled
    With treacle and my whole.

40

MY first we make, but never wish to keep ;
    My second has some silent letters
      through it ;
My whole, they say, is near us when
    we sleep,
    And I was much attached, in child-
      hood, to it.

41

ONE summer night,
'Neath the pale moonlight
   O'er the crested waves we sped ;
As on deck I lay,
I watched the spray
   And my starry first o'erhead.
My last I've heard,
Was the latest word
   That Marmion ever said ;
The flowing bowl
They filled from my whole
   And the wine was rich and red.

42

ON a sickly bush my first flowers bloomed;
My second many has entombed ;
Few see my whole until consumed.

43

THE office-seeker's attitude is arrogant and
    proud,
His mien is very haughty, and his voice
    is very loud ;
He 'll bow to no man's orders, by none
    he 'll be coerced,
Yet he always is delighted when he 's
    asked to serve my first.

His mind is ever working out his ava-
    ricious dreams ;
He burns my midnight second while he
    plans his wily schemes ;
He devotes himself, untiring, his ambitions
    to attain,
And he throws himself with fervor in my
    whole of the campaign.

44

MY first is rippled by each passing breeze,
It spreads its watery wastes from pole to
pole.
My next, a Greek philosopher's abode ;
For years he lived there happily.   My
whole —
Ay, there's the rub ! — sits proudly on
the bench,
And causes its constituents to blench.

45

DEMURE, modest, and meek,
    In my whole she rode by,
With my first on her cheek,
    And a smile in her eye.
And when she had passed,
    I said, " She 's a dear,
And her critic my last
    To say she is queer."

46

THE farmhouse stood by the flowery lane,
   Down in the meadow the cows were
      lowing ;
A soft breeze stirred the golden grain,
   And a pretty maid to my first was going.

A rustic swain came by that way,
   (She looked so winning, who could
      resist her ?)
She blushed like any rose in May,
   And turned my second when he kissed
      her.

But as she took her homeward path,
   Her anger rose toward her daring lover ;
While she trembled in her righteous wrath
   From my whole the drops were brim-
      ming over.

47

MY feathered first to merry tune
    Skims lightly o'er the blue lagoon ;
Though in another shape 't is found
    In darksome caverns under ground.

A doting mother named her son
    Gustave Orlando Algernon ;
And then she was extremely vexed
    To hear the boys call him my next.

My whole is very high and rare,
    It lives suspended in the air ;
In shape and color 't will outvie
    The most resplendent butterfly.

48

MY first we hear with groans ;
   My second is a bird ;
My whole's seductive tones
   Wandering Ulysses heard.

49

OF traitors Arnold was the worst,
Yet Englishmen call him my first.
My second comes to all good men
Who reach their threescore years and ten.

My whole was by a heathen horde
Exalted, worshipped, feared, adored ;
But fell to earth, and perished, prone,
By Hebrew courage overthrown.

50

MY sainted first we all adore when young ;
　　But when my first is old, we fear his
　　　malice.
My last's a liquid pleasant to the tongue ;
　　'T is found in a saloon or gay gin-
　　　palace.
The New York merchant, when his day's
　　work's past,
Would give my whole to ride home on
　　my last.

51

ALTHOUGH in Bible lore well versed,
Some call the Sixteenth Psalm my first.
A suitor for a lady plead,
But her stern father firmly said,
" Until you have more wealth amassed,
You cannot call yourself my last."
My whole, by enemies surrounded,
A clever riddle once propounded.

52

M Y second is a high degree ;
   It was my mother's name.
I 'm sure that you can guess my first,
   If you my last can claim.
My whole Poor Richard used to write,
And many still its wisdom cite.

53

THE dread mosquito's found the most,
They say, along the Jersey coast,
But where its bite is really worst
Is on my second of my first.
My whole was cheered with shouts of glee ;
Men fought like beasts, with yell and
     snort,
And ladies fair looked on to see
     The brutal sport.

54

IF we open my first,
　　We perceive it 's a jar.
My second, they say,
　　Is upholding the bar.
By something we hear
　　Very frequently said,
We are led to infer
　　That my total is dead.

55

ALTHOUGH my first was all his life
    ignored,
Above his cavillers his spirit soared ;
And with his unpraised prose and unread
    rhyme
He flung his genius in the teeth of Time.

My second, always eager to assail,
You 're often beaten, thereby hangs a tale ;
And often on your helpless prey you
    pounce,
The while half-muttered curses you
    pronounce.

My whole, for many tragedies to blame,
What crimes have been committed in thy
    name !
Wife-beating, dissipation, martyrs blind,
And ruined lives thy mention brings to
    mind.

56

THE lady was my first, and so
　　To kiss her made her vext;
Her hair was black as any sloe,
Her pretty curls waved to and fro,
　　I asked her for my next.
My whole, a wretch athirst for slaughter,
Preferred his ducats to his daughter.

57

I WATCHED my first essay her part,
She shone in histrionic art ;
While many stared, with bated breath,
I was my last almost to death ;
Even in the dark and stormy night
The sailor knows my whole is right.

58

MY first is Tartary's ruling prince ;
My second often makes us wince ;
My total we are apt to pass
Whene'er we see it in the glass.

59

MY first we may see when approaching
New York,
We often obtain it by means of a fork;
In its secret assistance the pupil delights,
The New Woman claims it as one of
her rights.

My second is dug by the farmer's sharp
spade,
But viewed with dismay in my lady's
brocade;
Attractive to mice, in a cake often found,
'T is seen in the old, and made in the
ground.

My whole may be easily guessed from
these rhymes;
I 'm sure you 've seen through it a great
many times.

60

ONCE on a time, a godly man
Lived in my first for a brief span;
A thousand men were, we are told,
Slain by my last in days of old.
My whole lies deep on the ocean's bed,
The pale remains of a monster dead;
And with never a thought of its being
    misplaced,
My lady allows it around her waist.

61

MY first is made of clay or gold ;
 'T is very hot or very cold.
 My second, though you brush away,
 You will turn back to it some day.
 The scullery-maid, to make things shine,
 Uses my whole, a powder fine.

62

THE American eagle is dear to some,
But my first before the bird must come;
The Spanish court looked on, aghast,
When brave Columbus sailed my last;
My uncle's fortune 's said to be
A very handsome legacy;
'T will be my whole if left to me. .

63

A FISHERMAN was heard to say
He had n't caught my first that day;
But cheerfully he said he reckoned
That he would catch my first my second.
My tuneful whole, the roses heard
All night: so Tennyson averred.

5

64

MY last is computed by means of my
first;
It is lost, spent, and wasted, but that's
not the worst.
It is taken and killed, 't is reduced to a
point,
And sometimes 't is dragging along out
of joint.
When my last comes for roses to bloom
in my first,
My whole is by poets repeatedly versed.

65

WITHIN my first for many a day
The beautiful Ginevra lay.
My second's made of iron or dough;
My whole is something that you
know.

66

MY first was oftentimes bestowed
 By lady fair on valiant knight,
And if you give it to a friend,
 Undoubtedly 't is right.

For sale along a city street
 My second often may be found ;
Costly yet small, they 're sometimes
  sold
 A dozen to the pound.

My third was worshipped by his tribe,
 O'er all his men he reigned supreme ;
Yet each has some one whom he thinks
 My third in his esteem.

My whole, an old Egyptian charm,
 A wretch demanded of his wife,
Which failing to receive, enraged,
 He took her life.

67

THOUGH hardly a path of glory,
  My first leads to the grave ;
Unless by giving my second
  Both life and health we save.

My third is of very small value,
  The favorite haunt of a mouse ;
My whole you will find in the kitchen
  Of every well-ordered house.

68

MY first's an article in daily use ;
My next 's a well-known bird, but not a
goose ;
My third's the name a poet gave to
night ;
My whole's a much applauded circus
sight.

69

MY first's a flowery, bowery place
    Where streamlets gently glide;
My second is exactly half
    Of Nanki-Poo's fair bride;
My whole's a kind of resinous gum,
Or a precious stone it is thought by
    some.

70

A LITTLE Quakeress is my first ;
  Her eyes are dropped, her lips are pursed.
A blush her cheek has overcast;
Her pearly teeth are in my last.
My whole upon the river's brink
Was seen by Mr. Bell, I think.

71

MY one and two Canova's fame prolongs;
My three is ivy-crowned on old
 Silenus;
My whole, I'm sure you will agree,
 belongs
To Massachusetts and the Milo Venus.

72

MY first is strong and cruel when in a
    rage ;
Sometimes it separates two loving hearts.
My last is quoted from an ancient sage ;
The tramp, when he perceives its teeth,
    departs.
My first is always present, but my last,
Though we recall it, is for ever past.
My whole's a merry game or ballad
    gay
The children and the organ-grinders
    play.

73

IN dark and stormy times, by God's decree,
 My first fell to the dust. A king was
  crowned,
So wise and just, by all the region round
Peaceful and blest my first was said to be.

Before his queen my second bends the knee,
 A German leader, for his skill renowned
 In bow or ball ; and with salute profound,
Among the lancers meets his vis-à-vis.

Niagara! I love thy thunderous roar,
 Thy mighty torrent dashing madly by,
  Thy fairy spray twinkling with dia-
  monds bright.
And standing, spell-bound, on the rocky
 shore
 I watch thy grandeur. Faintly I descry
  My shining whole, with rapturous
  delight.

74

MY first for industry
   Has achieved a great renown ;
A singer made my last
   In a simple cotton gown ;
Each Sabbath day, my whole
   Peals forth in many a town.

75

MY first is round and very thin,
　　You take it with your tea ;
My second every one must have,
　　It grows within a tree ;
History declares my whole was bare,
　　Which caused much misery.

76

ALTHOUGH I plead,
She firmly said
    My first, which dashed my dreams.
My second we
Admit to be
    Not always what it seems.

You may find my whole
In a golden bowl,
    And kings for it have striven ;
The pauper owns,
The miser loans,
    And the Pope to us has given.

77

MY second spoke my first, and it was
    handed down in history ;
Though you correctly guess my whole,
    't will still remain a mystery.

78

I SING my first. Come dirges and sad
    moans,
And wailings dire, and sobbing sighs and
    groans,
And blighted hopes, and swiftly dropping
    tears,
And dreary days, and long and lonely years.

I sing my last. Come mirth and laughter
    gay,
On with the festive dance till dawn of day !
Come merry madness, revelry, and sport,
And fickle Folly holding mimic court.

Copied from Shakespeare, whom it well
    defines,
My whole has strength and beauty in its
    lines.

79

ONE beautiful day in early May,
　　Some recreation wishing,
I took my creel and my rod and reel,
　　In my first I went a-fishing.

I chanced to pass a country lass,
　　I smiled as I espied her;
For with awkward air and a sheepish stare
　　My second walked beside her.

When the day was spent, I homeward
　　　went,
　　While the twinkling starbeams glistened;
'T was a glorious night, and with calm
　　　delight
　　To the song of my whole I listened.

6

80

MY first can never look you in the eye;
My second is of use in Copenhagen;
My whole's a land that millions occupy,
'T is partly christianized and partly
pagan.

81

MY first at times the sea-breeze gently
  stirs,
Again my first speeds foaming o'er the
  track
And wins the race.
                    My second stands among
An ancient line of noted characters;
A noble line, my second near the head.

My whole, a monarch absolute, controls
His subjects with despotic power and
  sway
Albeit they love him. If he speak or
  move,
They say, "Aha! my lord doth so
  and so."

And if he but express a wish, they fly
Instantly to obey his shrill behest.
Shakespeare avows he wears upon his
  brow
The very round and top of sovereignty.

82

MY first describes the widow's weeds,
The Ace of Spades, the melon's seeds;
My next we value in our hand,
The emblem of our native land;
My whole, the ancient story goes,
One day bit off a lady's nose.

83

I WANDERED long in deserts dry,
  Pure water was my quest;
And when it proved to be my whole
  That sparkled in the west,
My first and second better be
  Imagined than expressed.

84

WHEN Shakespeare's fair Viola wished
for a beard,
On my first, as my first we are told
she appeared ;
Of my second, King Solomon truly
declares
Her meat in the summer she duly
prepares ;
With blaring of trumpets and banging
of drums,
My whole in its splendor trium-
phantly comes.

85

THE hall was illumined,
  The darkness dispersed,
As my last through my whole
Came down from my first.

86

MY last is a stone,
  And my first is a fraud ;
Though it quiets a babe's moan,
Yet my last is a stone ;
My total is grown
  In a country abroad ;
My last is a stone,
  And my first is a fraud.

87

I WALKED across my first,
  With my second in my arms,
In hopes that I might find my whole
  At one of the near-by farms.

Success my efforts crowned,
  My whole came at my beck ;
I left my one and two, and said,
  '' Be sure to wring its neck.''

88

MY first by some old sage
  Was kept until it dried,
A season it remained
  And then 't was thrown aside.

My second and my third
  Has four legs and a head,
And three times every day
  We carry to it bread.

When in a railroad train
  At rattling speed we roll
From Boston to New York,
  The train goes by my whole.

89

MY first proclaims the night is past
And day has dawned. Hope tells my
   last.
My whole some take to quench their
   thirst,
And yet my whole adorns my first.

90

MY sweet first, with thy rosy cheek
And fair soft skin, 't is thee I seek ;
    By slaves thou shalt be served
If thou wilt come and stay with me ;
And if I can, I 'll surely see
    That thou art well preserved.

My next is good beyond a doubt,
Yet saving people throw it out,
    Or send it to a friend ;
My whole is used to cleanse and scrub,
Advertisements with pictured tub
    Its properties commend.

91

THE farmer shook his shrewd old poll,
As cleverly he drove my whole ;
Then by his appetite accurst,
Spent all my second at my first.

92

ALTHOUGH my first men shoot and eat,
  It is not always wild;
My second crowned with blossoms sweet
Is clambering o'er a rustic seat,
  Sweet Nature's graceful child.
My whole thrives best in tropic heat,
  Or where the climate's mild.

93

MY first a brute declined to cross ;
   The ladies scorn it when it 's past.
Brave heroes, now beneath the moss,
   Preserved my last unto my last.
My whole, in Rome's illustrious day,
Wrote the Æneid, so they say.

94

THERE once was a beautiful dancing-
   girl,
   Her lips and her cheeks were red ;
And in consequence of her graceful
   whirl,
   My first soon lost his head.

The noise of my second we shuddering
   hear,
   For oft where its rattle is found,
The serpent that bites is lingering near,
   And the adder that stings is around.

My whole is the color of quinces or
   gold,
   Of saffron or daffodil ;
It causes jealousy, we are told,
   And it makes us awfully ill.

95

MY first knaves brought to me a heap of
    gold ;
  Shuddering, I heard a voice out of
    my second ;
My whole was by an old Egyptian told,
  And fabulous by all my friends, 't is
    reckoned.

96

WHEN I'm my whole, I do not care
Whether the days be dark or fair;
   I do not care for crops or grain,
   For pipes or horses or champagne,
Or what I eat, or what I wear.

I care not though my friends declare
My first is calm.   I'm in despair.
   And cheerfulness I cannot feign
      When I'm my whole.

Consequent joys I'll gladly spare;
I'd rather be my last elsewhere,
   Haply within my own domain.
   And though I'm really not profane
I almost feel obliged to swear
      When I'm my whole.

97

MY first young Hamlet called the Ghost ;
  Upon my next the British host
  Fought Prescott's men with ball and
      blade ;
  Out of my whole are mountains made.

98

MY first hangs from the Congo trees,
Subject of many theories ;
Among the hills and mossy dells,
Among the wildwood brakes and fells,
'Neath winter skies and summer suns,
My noisy little second runs.
When rains their swelling torrents bring,
You 'll find my whole in every spring ;
And in my whole the great Shakespeare
Began and ended his career.

99

A HARROWING tale I'm about to relate
Of a beautiful maid and her horrible
fate.
The actors are three,
In this grim tragedy ;
So of course complications we all can
foresee.
And as each represents a particular rôle,
We'll call them my second, my first,
and my whole.
Now my whole was to wed
With my first, but instead,
To his horror, he found that the lady had
fled,
Though the gay marriage-tables already
were spread.
And on looking around
He very soon found
That my second was missing.　Of course
he had ground
To believe they'd eloped.　He stormed
and he frowned ;
He terribly cursed
Both my second and first,

Indeed I don't know which he rated the
worst.
Her mother just fainted away in despair;
Her papa from the depths of his big
easy-chair
Said, "Well, I declare
I don't know as I'd care
If she'd only gone off with a rich mil-
lionaire;
But my last for my son, I never could
bear."
My whole mounted a horse
And he followed their course,
Resolved that he'd rescue the lady by
force.
Half hoping she'd greet him with tears
and remorse;
He espied them afar! He o'ertook them
at length,
And he challenged my last to a trial of
strength.
The lady sat by
With a tear in her eye,
Being really unwilling that either should
die.

They fought and they sparred,
Until wounded and scarred,
Both gave up the ghost, like the cats of
    Kilkenny,
And instead of two lovers, my first
    had n't any.

PRINTED AT THE UNIVERSITY PRESS,
IN   CAMBRIDGE,   MASSACHUSETTS,
FOR STONE AND KIMBALL, PUBLISH-
ERS, NEW YORK, M DCCC XCVI

www.ingramcontent.com/pod-product-compliance
Lightning Source LLC
Chambersburg PA
CBHW022341020726
47500CB00004B/1221

* 9 7 8 3 3 3 7 3 8 8 3 4 8 *